The Fox And The Mermaid

Dee Carey

The Fox and the Mermaid
Copyright © 2023 by Dee Carey

ISBN: 978-1639457502 (sc)

ISBN: 978-1639457519 (e)

All rights reserved. No part of this publication may be reproduced, distributed, or transmitted in any form or by any means, including photocopying, recording, or other electronic or mechanical methods, without the prior written permission of the publisher, except in the case brief quotations embodied in critical reviews and other noncommercial uses permitted by copyright law.

The views expressed in this book are solely those of the author and do not necessarily reflect the views of the publisher, and the publisher hereby disclaims any responsibility for them.

Writers' Branding
(877) 608-6550
www.writersbranding.com
media@writersbranding.com

Contents

Acknowledgements vii
Cast of Characters ix
Prologue xi

Chapter 1: LIAM (fox) 1
Chapter 2: NEPTUNE 15
Chapter 3: MURTAUGH 31
Chapter 4: LIAM 39
Chapter 5: MURTAUGH 47
Chapter 6: MURTAUGH 57

This book is dedicated to

*my late husband, Bill (the love of my life) to
my children and grandchildren.*

Without them I would be lost.

Acknowledgements

Thanks to those whose' encouragement kept me continuing to write. I could not function without your aid. Special thanks to my critique partner, Steve Yates.

Cast of Characters

Chloe – Selkie who has been taken prisoner
Liam – A fox with no past
Murtaugh – A Druid priest
Aggy – A sea unicorn
Neptune – The King of the Sea
Arwan – A Questing Beast / a mortal man
Turlough – Blind King of Ireland
Moria - Sister of Arwan/wife of Blind King

Prologue

At the time before the events of man were recorded, the ancients comprised an oral history and were responsible for all the events both above the sea and beneath it.

As no name was given to these beings they were simply called "The Council."

When an event occurred that would endanger the inhabitants of those above and those below "The Council" would intervene, using whatever means they had at their disposal.

Chapter 1
....

LIAM (fox)

I watched an exquisite creature as she ran swiftly down the beach, her long legs taking powerful strides to escape the fiend chasing her. Bright red hair plumed behind her like a crimson cloak. She was a vision, more beautiful than any other woman I'd ever seen.

What chased her was the most ugly creature in all creation. He came running pell-mell down the lonely beach. His footfalls rebounded against the small stones, sending them scattering into the air. His voice was deep and throaty, uttering threats of terror. I'm fairly certain he's human, but his entire demeanor was evil and beast-like.

She was clearly frightened, but also fleet of foot. Racing ahead, she eluded him, his girth preventing her capture. He was too fat and too slow. Growling in frustration, he whipped his head from side to side in anger.

Abandoning the chase, he walked, muttering, back to the lone cottage on this wide stretch of beach. The door on the house was red, the same color as the lass's hair. It was the only hue to be seen. Everything else was covered with a dark pall. The stones were gray, the water the same. Even the grasses at the water's edge were gray, the sky overhead the same dingy color.

I'd only been on this beach a short time, maybe a month, and each day was as dark as the last. It was as if someone had sucked the joy and light out of the world. This land was dark. I'm sure there was a sun, as there was a difference between day and night. But that sun never shed its light on this solitary beach. What was the cause?

My senses were heightened. Was it my destiny to find the answer? Surely others were far more qualified? If this be true, why do I feel such a strong compulsion to rectify the situation? What could a fox do anyway? Often times I feel as if I am not really a fox at all. As if I were in the wrong skin. My memories of family are nonexistent. I remember not my mother or any siblings. It seemed I was placed in the meadow without a past. There never was a time that I did not feel lonely. Fortunately I'm not a pack animal, so was able to subsist on my own. Though in this dark land food was scarce.

Not so long ago, the meadow from whence I came was green and verdant. Well I remember the day when everything changed. The flowers wilted and died, the grasses turned a sickly green-gray. Trees were covered with choking dark vines, cutting off the life of pines, oaks and maples. The sky overhead, once a clear blue with a few white puffy clouds, grew instantly dark and ominous. It was likened to a curtain being drawn where all light was hidden.

I was frightened and thought I would be safer closer to the bay that opened to the Irish Sea. It was the opening of Ireland to the world. Surely there could be nothing wrong there? How wrong I was. Even here, the land was somber and bleak. This was a land with no hope. Still I felt there was something I could do. But what?

I did not have long to ponder the question when I heard a high-pitched, but faint, whinny. Why would there be a horse on the shore? I walked in every direction, and found nothing. Nothing, save the fat ugly man, had left their mark. No tracks of any kind. Again I heard the sound. This time it was nearer. It seemed to be coming from the rocks near a tide pool. As the tide was going out, the rocks next to the pool seemed nearly dry. I walked out onto the wet pebbles. They were uncomfortable against my paws, some so tiny they worked their way between my toes. I couldn't continue far like this, but again the cry sounded and I put aside the pain and ventured on.

As I peered over the edge of the pool I saw a sea horse valiantly trying to escape to the open water. I reached down and picked him up by his dorsal fin and held him gently with my mouth. He was white, an unusual color for a sea horse. It was then I noted he had a gold horn right in the center of his forehead. I'd never seen a sea horse of this size, let alone one with a horn. He was not large, but at least an inch bigger than most sea horses. I immediately felt a strong connection to the creature and an instant bond formed between us.

This day was becoming more and more bizarre. Did my feeling toward the woman and the sea unicorn serve the same purpose? I knew deep within my soul that my destiny was unfolding and the time for action was near. I hoped and prayed the part I should play would be made clearer to me. For I had no idea how the darkness could be banished.

Once I set him in the sea, he dove and swam away. I felt strangely bereft.

Both of my discoveries of the day were gone. Perhaps I was reading too much into the circumstance? Downhearted, I headed back to the shore to find lodging for the night. Though the grasses were dark and gray, they most likely would provide some protection from the elements.

I made myself a nest of sorts by tamping the reeds and then settled down to rest. It was then I heard a fearful roar, followed by a hiss coming directly for my hiding spot. Did it see me? Or smell me? Whatever it was, it didn't sound friendly. I peered through the grasses and beheld the strangest creature I ever saw. It had a large snake-like head, moving it from side to side, and a long, forked tongue thrusting it outward, tasting the air. Further down the animal's body I noted it was spotted like a leopard before morphing into the back of a lion. It stood on deer hooves and again roared and pushed its head into the reeds.

I barely escaped as I ran from my hiding place. It followed me down the beach. I ran until my paws bled. It had my scent and hiding was not an option. Its long, loping strides quickly caught up to me. The snake hissed and sunk its fangs into my flank. Then it whipped me around and stomped upon my body with the sharp, cloven hooves. I knew I was going to die and today was the day it would happen. My ribs were broken, I could barely breathe. Letting my body grow limp, I noted the creature seemed to lose interest. Apparently it wanted a fight and not acquiring one, it'd left me there on the beach to die.

And die I would have, had not the beautiful woman found me.

~ ~ ~

CHLOE

Why? Why? What does he get out of hurting everything living thing that crosses his path? Though he's held me captive since he found my skin, I did not expect his level of cruelty to continually rise.

This poor fox is barely alive. Somehow, I feel compelled to save him. As if he is part of my destiny. Only good can come from aiding him. I gathered him up in my arms and took him to the willow bower far from the cottage. *Arwan never goes there, the fox will be safe.*

Gently, I placed the fox in the bed I created for myself when I wished to be alone. The poor creature was whimpering. His hunch was swollen from the bite and his ribs were clearly broken from the sharp hooves of the Questing Beast.

"Please, please help me."

I looked up. Who had spoken? There was no one other than me and the fox within the bower. Yet I heard not actual speech, simply a voice in my head.

"Did you speak to me, friend fox?"

"Yes," he replied weakly.

Perhaps I should not have been surprised. After all I was a Selkie, and my husband a Questing Beast. Why wouldn't a fox have the power to communicate?

The fox lowered his head and his eyelids fell. He was failing fast. I covered him with willow branches and ran to the edge of the sea. I grabbed two handfuls of seaweed and raced back to him.

I could not rouse him.

Taking a cloth and some clean water I always kept in my secret hideaway, I started to clean his wounds. The venom was quickly coursing through his veins.

Taking my shelling knife I scraped the area around the wound clear of fur. Sucking the bite, I spat out the poison. It was as bitter as gall. I did this several times, until I was certain all I tasted was blood. The fox sighed and fluttered open his eyes.

"Thank you."

He was too weak to say more, and, relaxing, his breathing became even. Packing his other wounds with the seaweed, I felt confident he would survive. But his survival was not the only problem. Should Arwan discover him, he would kill the fox. I could not be certain my husband would not decide to seek him out and search more diligently. It was clear only Arwan could have caused the damage. This small woodland creature that was not usually found seaside would have to be well hidden, until he was well.

I needed more help if I was to save the fox. I couldn't be with him all the time. But who? All I knew were my sea friends. Somehow I would have to reach them. The tide would not go out until morning, perhaps Aggy would return to the pool when the tide comes in and remain until I can speak with him. I wish there was some way I could reach him now. Going back to the cottage was my only option at the moment.

Filled with despair, I sank to the beach and sobbed. I should have been more silent. Arwan heard me. He emerged from the cottage, his features cemented in a permanent scowl.

"What are you doing out here? Get back in the house."

"Arwan, please, only a moment more? I'm watching the stars."

"All right, you're useless anyway."

I knew I dare not tarry long, but I had to get control of my feelings, else I cause further harm to the fox by being too injured myself to help him. Crouching on the pebbles, my shoulders shuddered as I tried to control myself. Sobbing convulsively I could not seem to stop. I wept for the fox, for the land, and for myself.

Would that my tears were a soothing balm, that I could heal the fox and my own pain as well. Giving in to self-pity would not solve anything. I walked to the water's edge, knelt, and splashed my face. Having gained control of myself, I rose and went to the bower wherein the fox slept.

The poor creature looked pitiful, but content. It was clear he trusted me. I petted him gently. He woke and looked at me with trusting eyes, as if I were his savior. How I hoped and prayed that I would be.

"I have to leave you now but I shall return in the morning."

"Nooo, please stay with me. I shall perish without you."

"Nay, little friend, I'll not let that happen, but for now you must remain hidden. I will bring you food and care for your injuries. You will be safe here, do not fear."

"But I do not even know your name. Mine is Liam."

"I am Chloe. Do not fear, I will protect you. Rest now, and I will see you on the morrow. I will return as soon as he leaves."

~ ~ ~

MURTAUGH O'BRIEN (Druid)

I pray I am up to this task. Never has the duty been more profound. How in the name of all that's revered could this darkness descend so quickly and endure for so long? We all thought it was a temporary situation. None of us, not Merlin, not Neptune, not even the High King of Ireland could explain the phenomenon. It is not as if we could implore the sun. Though she had the power, she was not like us. I dare say she cared not upon whom her rays descended.

The day is dawning, though it is difficult to discern, as it is nearly as dark as night.

Turlough O'Connor had served as High King for quite some time now. When he took the throne he was a good and just king. After his accident, however, he became a different man entirely. He was blind and angry. Very angry.

And so it was, I was summoned by the Ancient Order of the Druids, to see if I could shed some light on the situation. Alone, I was helpless. There was nothing I could do. Apparently the Druids foresaw the situation as the High Council informed me I was just a single part of the plan to illuminate the land once again. King Turlough had been summoned as well and was to assist in the endeavor. I had just settled myself on the beach, when a carriage drove up beside me. The king stepped out, led by a large thin greyhound. The animal appeared to have the situation in control as he nudged his charge over to my side.

I bowed as was due his station. "Good day, Your Highness. I am pleased to have been chosen for this honor."

Turlough nodded and turned his head in my direction. "Thank you. I am sorry to say since I cannot see you, I have no knowledge of who you are."

"Highness, I am known as Murtaugh O'Brien. I have long been a Druid and wander throughout the country trying assist those who might need my aid."

"That is very selfless of you. Quite commendable." The words were laced with venom. He appeared angry at having to be in my presence. Reaching out to touch his dog, he turned from me. He seemed to have no interest in speaking with me about the problem that faced us. If he wasn't going to provide some insight why did he bother to come? The man was a puzzle to me. I've known others who lacked sight that were not so self- absorbed. Some, in fact, showed extraordinary skills and were little hampered by their vision lack. One would think a king would realize, that though he could not see, he possessed other attributes that would assist him in the governing of his people. Turlough was bitter and not disposed to aiding me. I could only hope the High Council had another selected to help me.

I found it strange that I'd been sent to a seemingly deserted beach. Was I to find a mermaid? The High Council does not possess a sense of whimsy so that probably is not the case.

I paused to ponder the situation and though I knew somehow someone would be sent to join me in this endeavor, I was at a loss as to where this someone might be. Looking about, the only dwelling I saw appeared deserted. There was no one tending the small garden beside the cottage and the goat alongside the building needed milking. Venturing closer, I heard muffled sobs from within. I knocked on the red door. No one answered, and the sobbing hushed. Someone was fearful to allow entrance to an unknown. Usually a wise practice. However, the gulping sobs tore at my heart. I could hear it was a woman.

"Miss, please allow me to help you. I mean you no harm. My name is Murtaugh and I am a Druid. I've been sent by the High Council to this shore and I know not exactly what for what purpose. Perhaps it is to aid you. Please open the door."

For a time there was no sound, then I heard the wood scrape against the dirt floor. A very beautiful woman, whose face was streaked with tears, stood within the doorframe. Her eyes were swollen nearly shut.

"Are-Are you like a priest?"

"Yes, my child, I am a Druid Priest. How can I help you?"

This poor woman was cut, bruised, and battered. I'd never seen a person so badly beaten. It was a wonder she was able to stand. She was hesitant to disclose her situation, yet she accepted I was a priest and then opened the door fully. She tried to speak, but her sobbing made it difficult for me to understand her.

"Calm yourself, my lady," I said. "Just tell me slowly and we will see what we can do about your problem."

She sat upright and drew in a deep breath and then proceeded to tell me what had happened to her.

"My husband beats me and tries to kill every living being that crosses his path. He is truly some kind of a demon. I have never seen him as the beast he becomes, but I've seen the damage he inflicts. Only last night he bit a small fox and nearly killed him. When I found the poor creature on the beach I tended his wounds and hid him."

"I understand your compassion, my child, but why are you crying now?" Though the deep sobbing stopped, tears still poured from her eyes.

"As I was caring for the fox I stayed out longer than Arwan wanted me to and he struck me as I entered the cottage. He then proceeded to whip, slap, and punch me until I was senseless. I've only now just awakened and am behind in my chores. He will beat me again if I do not complete them in the time he thinks I should."

"Where is he now?"

"I know not. Each day he leaves at dawn and returns at sunset. I must provide our food and care for the cottage. He contributes nothing. Nothing but my fear, which he seems to relish."

"So we are safe from his presence for a while?" I did not want to encounter the fiend before I was truly prepared. Though I'd lived centuries I'd never been trained as a warrior. Fighting was not my forte.

"Yes," she replied, "He will not return until sundown. He's never altered from his pattern."

"Well, that's good. I wouldn't like to be surprised."

"He is definitely a creature of habit. I must get to my chores, as his habit of beating me will not alter either." She stood and reluctantly walked toward the cottage.

"Wait, I'll help you with your chores and then we can see to the condition of the fox." Things were becoming clear in my mind. The fox was as much a part of this as both the lass and I.

She turned, smiling, and said, "Your help is most welcome. I've never had anyone assist me. Thank you."

~ ~ ~

CHLOE

Though the man was not a warrior, I felt certain he would protect me. Having known no other man than Arwan, the Druid's behavior was unusually kind. I'd never experienced kindness before. It was a feeling of complete euphoria. A feeling as freeing as when I was a seal beneath the ocean waves.

Between the two of us we completed the chores in record time. The rest of the day until sunset was mine. Mine to do with as I wished. And what I fervently wished for was to see to the fox. How I prayed he would still be alive. He could easily have succumbed to his injuries.

"Murtaugh, thank you for helping me. It is most appreciated. You have given me a gift. Now may we see to the fox?"

"Of course. Have you any mendicants? I only carry a small portion of willow bark, which might relieve his pain, but nothing to cure infection."

The Druid was apparently lost in thought as he wandered in front of me. He stopped abruptly and turned. "I guess I got ahead of myself. Am I going the right direction?"

"Almost," I shouted over the sound of the waves.

"Veer to the left by the willow. He's in there." Murtaugh smiled and stopped, allowing me to catch up with him.

"I pray he's lasted the night. He was sorely wounded." My heart was filled with trepidation. I'd done all I knew how to do, but the creature was teetering on death. Pushing aside the low-hanging branches of the willow, I ushered the cleric into the bower.

"My lass, you have created a veritable haven in here. It is as sumptuous as a castle."

Laughing, I shook my head. While it was comfortable, it was most certainly not sumptuous. The fox lay on the bed I made for him. His eyes were bright and clear. When he saw me, I felt his voice in his head.

"Thank you, Chloe, I'm much better. Who is the man with you?"

"You need not fear him, he's a Druid who believes you and I are to join him in the mission to rid the land of the darkness."

Murtaugh frowned. "Who are you talking to? And what do you mean I believe I am to aid in this endeavor? We were chosen, all of us. What I believe is of no consequence."

"I only reply to the voice in my head, which is, in fact, the fox. Perhaps because he can communicate is the reason he also was selected?"

"Of course. I do not always understand the wisdom of the Council, but they do not handle matters frivolously. No matter how or why he is picked we must aid him."

"I've packed his wounds in seaweed, which will draw out any putrefaction. I do not think enough time elapsed between his beating and my aiding, him that would have allowed deep infection to set in." I knew the Druid was skeptical of my talents as a healer, but living beneath the sea afforded me knowledge I might never have known otherwise.

Gently I removed the now-dry seaweed and examined the wounds. The redness was greatly reduced and the injuries no longer wept. I reached down to touch his ribs and he did not flinch. Apparently they were only bruised, not broken. This is a good sign.

"I fare much better this morn, my lady. Thanks to your tender care."

"You are most welcome, Liam."

I found the fox's comment quite touching. I smiled. He sounded as if he were a knight wounded in a tournament, not an abused woodland creature. Could it be that the fox might be the guise of another being, much like myself? That might explain my strong attraction to him. Otherwise, I was simply daft.

"Liam?" Murtaugh replied. "Is that the name you gave the fox, or did he tell you that was his name?"

"He told me it is his name. Does it have any significance to our cause?"

"None that I am aware of. However, I was directed to find William who will lead us to the light."

"Surely you know Liam means William in Gaelic."

"Yes, yes, of course. I'd forgotten as I use little of the old tongue these days. The darkness has driven much knowledge from my mind."

"Please pardon my forwardness, but I feel we should give Liam another day to rest and heal. He seems fine, but overtaxing his strength could be his undoing. And perhaps ours."

"Well, as this day is almost at a close perhaps we should wait until the morning tide comes in."

~ ~ ~

AGGY (sea unicorn)

"This is the best part of the day. My favorite of all times. The tide lifts you up, and the experience is almost spiritual. And I get to visit with my bestest friend in the whole world. Chloe is so kind to me. She saves the finest morsels of her food for me. I am not really fond of the food I find in the sea. I guess it's funny since that's where I live. At least most of the time. I can breathe on land and in the sea, but I can't stay on land all the time. I don't know why it is, it just is, and I don't have any family to tell me why. I guess I'm the only unicorn seahorse in the world. That's probably why I talk aloud to myself so much.

"Oh, here comes the wave that takes me to my tide pool. Just relax and let it put you right in the pool. Wow what a ride. And there she is. My Chloe, my dearest friend. She doesn't look too good.

"What happened to you?" I asked Chloe.

"Why are you all bruised? Did you fall? Does it hurt?"

"Aggy, it matters little, and only hurts a little. We need your help."

"We? Who's we?" Just then, I saw a man in a rustic gray robe coming toward the pool.

Chloe stepped aside and introduced me to the stranger. "This is Murtaugh. He's a Druid and he has come to help bring back the light to world."

"You mean he can make the sun shine on my pool so the water is warm?" I really like the warm water.

"Yes, but no, he is going to drive the gray from our shores. I'm going to help him and Liam."

"Who's Liam?"

"He's a fox Arwan attacked and I have nursed him to health. Liam is part of the plan too."

"Plan? Does my Lord Neptune know of this plan? I have to tell him you are hurt you know."

"Yes," the Druid interjected, "You must inform him of Chloe's injuries. You must also tell him he is wanted here on land for a time. He too is part. It will take many to solve this problem."

"Okay," I said, "I'll tell him."

Chloe leaned over my pool. "Please no, Aggy, if Arwan learns I've told anyone about the beatings I shall not survive the next one."

"But I hasta, it's my job."

The man in the gray robe leaned toward me. He shook his head. "I will handle the matter with Neptune." Chloe did not hear him as he spoke very softly. He signaled to me I was to proceed as if I were reporting as I should.

Swiftly I dove into the depths to find the King of the Sea. I am important. I take messages from land to the King. That's me Aggy the Messenger. But it's kinder funny I goes into the deep sea, but not to find the King? So I wanders around for a bit, wondering what the Druid guy really wants.

Then I sees King Neptune himself. He's plowing through the water with the force of a whale. The waves he makes are as tall as a house. I can tell, he's mad. I guess I better do as the robed man said, so I swim away from the mighty King. Back to the safety of my tide pool.

They're still there sitting beside my special haven. She's still crying—the Druid man is trying to comfort her—and the fox is just sitting next to her with his paw on her leg.

I calls out to them, and they all peer over the rim of the pool. The fox says, "Hi, Aggy" like we was old friends. Only known him a day, but I feels like we is friends, good friends.

Chapter 2
....

NEPTUNE

I emerged from my sea alongside of little Aggy's private swimming spot. The Druid, who I'd not seen in many years, had his arm around one of my seals who had lost her skin to a man. Now she served as the monster's slave wife. I was not fond of the situation, but the rules were made and I, too, must adhere to their tenets.

I had hurried from the depths once the Council summoned me. His sonorous voice bellowed, urging me to come at once. He did not state why, and I felt danger in his tone. As he was on land and I was in the water, the usual method of communication did not suffice. Yet, it was as if he screamed in my head, the sound vibrating off my skull. For whatever reason he called to me, and I knew it was no small matter.

When I saw Chloe, I became enraged, turning the calm water into a roiling sea with waves many feet higher than I'd ever created before I demanded answers.

"Who dares treat one of my subjects in this manner? Murtaugh, who is responsible for this travesty?"

"My Lord Neptune, I fear this is the work of an evil greater than any we have yet faced." *How I pray that this too will end well.*

"Have you been called?"

"I have, but I must tell you not all of us so called, are eager for this mission to succeed."

How could this be? "All chosen by the Order of Ancient Druids are sworn to undertake each mission with zeal. Who would dare ignore the Ancient Druids Commandments?"

Rage filled my countenance. Who could this fool be?

Murtaugh was slowly walking toward the cottage Chloe called home. The lass was engaged in a conversation with my messenger and the fox. Had they also been called to eradicate the darkness? What special skills do these possess?

As I cannot easily walk on land, I bellowed, "Murtaugh, get back here and tell me who this fiend is."

The Druid walked, at the pace of a snail, toward me. It was clear he didn't want to reveal the traitor.

I roared, "Are you protecting this evildoer? What is your gain in this?"

"There is naught for me to gain. Like the rest, I, too, suffer from the constant darkness. I hesitate only because it is hard for me to believe anyone, let alone a king, would wish others to suffer merely for their own gratification."

"A King? You call me traitor?" I spat the words out like an overcooked biscuit. My blood was near to boiling, lava in my veins. Throwing down my trident, I watched it scatter the pebbles on the shore into a shower of gravel.

The Druid then rushed to my side and placed his hand over my arm to calm me. "No, no, Neptune, not the King of the Sea, the Blind King of Ireland."

"What is the reason for this foolhardy act? Why would anyone wish to damn an entire land to be dark and ominous?"

I could not believe a regent would treat his people so callously. I take pride in serving my subjects and attending to their needs. Though I was unaware of Chloe's abuse, trust that I will rectify the situation as soon as possible. No one should be treated in such a manner such as the poor lass has been.

Collecting myself, I went over the situation in my mind. How was I to combat this evil? What was the cause for it? Furthermore, why was the king of this land so opposed to returning light to his subjects? Perhaps he knew something I did not. Would interference in the matter make it worse? Did the regent actually have his people in mind when he appeared to be uncaring?

The Druid, who among us was the only one who spoke directly with the Council, seemed to have settled into a deadly calm. Does he have some of the answers?

As it seemed to be the only way to get the cleric's attention, I yelled, "Murtaugh, come to the edge of the shore with me. We need to form a solid plan before we undertake this monumental problem. I must know the strengths and weaknesses and special skills each possesses."

The priest turned and motioned the others to join us. I addressed the group.

"Liam, Aggy, Chloe, are you fit enough to handle this mission? This is no small task set before us. If any feel they cannot participate fully, let them speak now."

I looked over carefully the group before me. Chloe, though beaten and bruised, appeared determined. Liam, the injured fox, appeared ready to take on whatever task I set before him. The Druid, of course a man of dedication, seemed well prepared to do what was required. Even little Aggy appeared eager to proceed.

The sea unicorn was shaking in anticipation. I felt sorry that I could not assign him a monumental task. "Aggy, you are most important in this undertaking. You, as always, are my trusted messenger. It will be your duty to swiftly transmit information from the land to the sea."

The Druid stared at me as if I were incorrect in my instruction. "You feel that I am somehow remiss?"

Murtaugh sighed and shook his head. "Not at all, Your Highness, I was merely acknowledging your wisdom in choosing to speak to the smallest first. Most considerate."

"Aggy has served me long and well. I would do nothing to demean him." Chloe stood and moved to my side.

"Neptune, how am I to assist in this endeavor? I dare not leave for an extended period of time. He would kill me if I were gone overnight."

"Have no fear, precious one, you need not worry over Arwan. Ever again. Not only will you be gone overnight, you will be gone from his life forever."

"Can I go home, Majesty?"

"We shall see, my dear, we shall see."

The fox moved close to her side and leaned his head against her. There was more to this woodland creature than was first apparent. I sensed there was more than the return of the light to this situation. Something perhaps only the fox was aware of.

~ ~ ~

LIAM

I do not know why I am so drawn to this woman. Though she is quite beautiful, we are not of the same kind. Not only am I enchanted by her, I feel compelled to assist her in whatever manner I can. If it is for the good of this blighted land, so be it, but simply to be in her company is a gift. One I shall treasure always.

I had to draw myself away from her. Neptune was saying something I knew I was supposed to be paying attention to, yet Chloe was far more interesting.

Neptune raised his voice. "Listen, little fox, you, too, are part of this mission. It will serve you well to you take heed of what I'm saying."

The King of the Sea was angry with me and rightly so. I hung my head and begged his pardon.

"Sire, I am truly sorry. I will give you all of my attention."

The King turned his head sharply, a look of confusion covering his features. "Is that you, my fuzzy friend?" It was apparent Neptune had never experienced this type of communication.

"Yes, my King."

"If this be so, can you tell me what other special talent have you that the Druids would select you for this mission?"

Certain, not only of my skill, but confident I could aid in this endeavor. Cunning as most foxes are, I excelled at stealth. I was able to move in a manner that none could discern my presence.

"Sire, I can enter and observe without a single soul knowing I was ever there. I can listen to the plans of others and relay the conversation to those who would need the information, without those observed ever knowing they were overheard. I feel that this might be a valuable asset."

"Quite so, little fox. This truly is a worthy skill," the King replied, nodding sagely. He turned and placed his attention on Chloe. "And you, young lady, what can you contribute?"

Chloe's lower lip trembled. "I'm not certain, my lord, the only talent I possess is to learn very quickly. Once I am shown something, I never forget it. I can memorize mazes and the currents and eddies of the water." So many changes had occurred in her short life, she was frightened of what might be required of her, and thus belittled her own gifts.

The King nodded, a pleased expression on his face. Apparently the lass had provided whatever it was he felt he needed. I was certain deep within my heart she was more than capable. Whatever was placed before us, we would accept and complete in a most expeditious manner. I knew she would alter my fate. I know not how, only that it is a simple fact. We met for a reason.

King Neptune was frowning and rubbing his hands through his long white beard. He looked at all of us gathered before him and spoke, none too softly. "I am giving each of you a part of this plan. All the parts will work together, yet be carried out separately. Do you all understand?"

Each of us nodded, save the Druid. He appeared annoyed and turned his back on the small group.

"Neptune, who has given you the authority to head this mission?" the cleric inquired over his shoulder.

"I am the King. Why wouldn't I have the authority?" Neptune scowled at the Druid, his trident clenched tightly in his right hand, his left drawn back as if to strike Murtaugh. I walked to the edge of the water, looked up at the giant king, and said, "Sire, perhaps the Druid means he has more information. I'm sure he doesn't doubt your abilities"

"No, no, I did not mean you are less than capable," Murtaugh replied. "I simply inquire if you have spoken to the council. I don't believe you have."

The King rose even higher from the sea. "What gives you reason to believe that?" It seemed the priest was baiting him. But to what end?

Murtaugh shook his head, as if to say, *Even a dullard would understand.*

I was at a loss, I knew I was to be a part of a grand scheme, but had no idea what the plan should be.

"Master Druid, have you direction from the council? Is there something I must do?"

Again the King of the Sea rose and called out, "Yes, *Master Druid*, have you the plan? Does it differ vastly from what I have told you? Or is there another method I am unaware of?"

"Neptune, the plan is not the problem. What you have laid out is perfect. The problem is we have to arrange our method to fit the Druid direction. I merely wanted to know if you know of this."

"Murtaugh, this is not the first time I've aided the Council. Their instructions are clear to me."

I was confident the two would come to a viable solution. Though both were hardheaded, they would consider the people effected before anything for their own gain. Both men were true leaders.

I looked up at the Sea King and bowed slightly. "Your Royal Highness, I am prepared to do your bidding."

The King smiled down upon me, a hint of amusement in his glance. He knew I was placating the Druid.

Chloe drew alongside me and stood before the king. "I, too, am ready to undertake the task." Again the regent smiled. He knew we would do whatever he deemed necessary.

~ ~ ~

CHLOE

We stood like soldiers awaiting orders, each assigned a task. I was to accompany Liam into the Irish's king's castle. Somehow both the Sea King and the Druid felt we must know the location of each room and the entire layout of the structure. Liam was to listen to the blind King's private talks to see if he is truly concerned with eradicating the darkness or if for some reason wishes to retain it.

Fortunately the castle was not far distant. We could reach it before nightfall if we hurry.

I was growing fearful. It was drawing nigh to sunset. I wished to be gone before Arwan's return. Nudging the fox, I tilted my head to indicate I needed to leave. He looked up at me, a question in his glance. Pointing to the setting sun, I made him understand. I did not wish to anger the king by speaking directly to him, else he think I am but a foolish woman.

"Majesty, we must leave quickly, else the beast return. We understand what is required and wish to get underway."

The King dismissed us, and we set out. This was my freedom as well as a mission for the land. Throwing my arms skyward, I danced on the shore. To never have to face Arwan was a gift I never thought to receive. Liam loped along side of me and we quickly left the shore.

"I'm free Liam, free. Can you believe it? Somehow I know this is just a beginning for us. You are my destiny, I'm sure of it."

We ran upward toward the wide green meadow. The grass was softer on my feet than the rough pebbles on the shore. It was like stepping on a green cloud. Liam, too, was exhilarated he ran, his nose to the ground in search of a field mouse. Suddenly he rose high in the air and pounced on a hapless rodent. As he devoured his meal, I looked all about us. Things here on the meadow were far different than they are at the beach. Ahead was a thicket, not quite a forest, but the brush would provide us cover should we need it. The densely foliaged area seemed to go on endlessly. We walked and walked, until I felt I could not take another step. I fell in exhaustion and hunger. The fox would not allow me to stop

"Chloe, we are so close, please hang on just a little longer." He then led me to a nearby stream and bid me to drink. I did so and refreshed was able to continue.

After several hours, the massive castle came into view ahead of us. It stood high on a bluff. Its location was built for protection. A structure designed to be secure from attack. *How are we to enter undetected?*

Liam nudged me and indicated I was to crouch low to the ground and follow him. He led me around to the rear of the building to an entrance that was clearly near the kitchen. The scents were enticing as I'd not eaten the entire day.

"Chloe, I know you are hungry, but try to calm your stomach for a few moments more. Take some berries from that bush over there until we can find more satisfying fare."

I reached for the berries and saw a woman emerge carrying a small basket. Quickly, I drew back and hid behind the foliage. She reached for a berry so close to me, I feared she would mistake my nose for what she sought. In short order she completed her gathering and left. Several others began to enter the kitchen door as well. Liam tugged at my skirt, and I followed hopefully to blend in with the other servants.

The fox moved in such a manner as not to be seen at all. I was astounded with the size of the place. People seemed to be everywhere. It was strange there was so little light. No sconces on the wall and only foul-smelling tallow candles provided illumination. Never had I seen so many people, each of them about their various tasks. My attire was similar so I appeared to fit in, but I, too, needed a task. I noted several individuals cutting up vegetables. It looked to be a task anyone could perform and not a special endeavor. I moved to the large cutting area and took up a knife and began to pare a turnip. A heavy-set woman moved along side of me.

"Yer new, aren't ye, dearie? Let me show you an easier way to peel a turnip. Tis best to dip them in the scalding water, rather than trying to scrape the hide off the thing. Here, let me show you."

She took the root into her hand and set it in a large ladle. Plunging the vegetable into the hot water, she then removed it and dipped it into cold water. Then she took it and eased the outer skin from the turnip. I marveled at how many hours I scraped at them when I could have cleaned them in half the time.

"Ye see now, you'll have a bushel clean in less time than it takes to tell it." She wiped her hands on her apron and turned to another chore. I continued to clean the vegetables until the heavy-set woman clapped her hands and said, "Never mind what is needed for tomorrow, tis time to serve today's meal."

The women around me dissipated nearly into thin air. I followed them out into the large hall off the kitchen where some were involved in serving. Others vanished, likely to other duties. I took advantage and left the main area to scout the entire castle. At the end of the hall was a staircase leading to an upper level. There were no visible torches to light the way. This could be dangerous. I drew back into the shadows when I saw a small man appear surrounded by several men and a large dog. The dog walked alongside the sumptuously dressed man, never allowing his body to break contact with him. The dog was leading him.

The other men obviously had traversed the way many times as it did not appear they needed a light to direct them.

My task was not to listen to the men, so I continued on feeling my way by touching the wall. I found several small rooms, no doubt sleeping areas. I did not venture into these as they would not interest Murtaugh, so I ventured further. Descending the stairs, I came into an area that was better lit, however the improvement was slight.

I wondered how people were able to complete their tasks in such low light. It was clear the blind king did not wish to suffer alone. His malady was shared by those who served him. This must have something to do with the darkness that covered the land. But this was not my task. 'Twas mine to map the castle. Not an overly large structure, yet built to withstand the most horrific siege. The walls were thick and the battlements well hidden. The place was surrounded on three sides by both water so any assault would be easily thwarted. The portcullis on the far side of the drawbridge was of heavy oak and iron. It would not easily be breached.

In short order, I had memorized the interior layout of the entire castle. Surely the King of the Sea would be desirous of the placement of the battlements and how large the outside areas are. As there was little light inside I had some trouble finding an exit to the roof. I climbed a winding narrow staircase until I bumped my head against a seemingly low ceiling. Pushing against the wood, I found it gave way slightly. An overhead opening. I pushed with all my might and finally opened a hatch onto the roof. From this vantage point, I was able to see the entire configuration of the castle's buildings: the practice yard, the stables, and where the men were billeted. The area in the bailey that was designated to a marketplace, where vendors plied their wares. All clearly laid out before me.

It was with great pride I accomplished my task as I was directed. I'd stolen a scrap of parchment from the library and set the map to it. Carefully I rolled it up, placed it my skirt, and returned to the kitchen, where many workers were cleaning up the vestiges of the last meal. I blended in and took to scouring a large pan with sand and a coarse brush. Nearly finished with the work, the servants left, one by one. The cook removed her apron, put in on a peg on the wall, and nodded good-bye to me. Then I extinguished the last flickering candle and left the room.

~ ~ ~

LIAM

I walked quietly along the darkened halls, picking up the scent of the dog I followed. The animal led its master to two large oaken doors. The guards alongside the regent each reached to open the portal. The heavy wood creaked as the doors opened. Before them was a long crimson carpet. Near the end stood a massive chair upholstered in a midnight fabric. It held a look of luxury.

This blind king was a pampered man. The dog stopped, and the king reached out to touch the chair. He sat and rose his chin as if he had reminded himself not to continually look down as he did not wish to appear blind.

A small nervous man appeared from behind the large chair. He leaned over the regent and whispered to the King. I would have to get closer. It would not be an easy task. There was little furniture, thus fewer places to hide.

The King could not see me, but the other man could if he chose to look. I backed up close to the wall and hid behind a low-hanging tapestry. The little man glanced furtively all around the room. It was clear the man was frightened, of what I knew not.

"Sire," he ventured, "There are two men waiting to see you. Shall I show them in?"

The King nodded and waved the man away. I took advantage of the man's departure and moved silently beneath the skirted throne. There I would be privy to the private conversations of anyone conferring with the King. I would be completely hidden and comfortable as well. The luxurious carpet that led to Turlough's seat also extended beneath it. My listening post was warm and dark. In fact it was altogether too comfortable. I'd fallen asleep and missed the king's conversation.

I peered beneath the fabric and noted the room was as dark as a moonless night. In the dark I found my way out, following the scents of food. I'd not eaten this day and filling my belly was my first priority.

I am smaller than most of the dogs, but I was able to blend in and secure some food scraps for myself. My hunger satisfied, I resigned myself to the fact I would learn nothing this day. Returning to the throne room, I settled into my cozy hiding place.

~ ~ ~

CHLOE

My chore for the council completed, I searched the main hall for Liam. He was nowhere to be seen. It was agreed we would meet in a dark corner of the room where we would be unseen. But he was not there or anywhere I could see. Had he been captured? He was a small fox and carried no weapons. What could have happened to him?

I had little time to ponder as the cook approached me.

"Come on, dearie, it's time to serve the main meal." She directed me back to the kitchen and instructed me to fillet some eels. Though they were sea creatures I never liked them. Over the years, many times they tortured me thus skinning them and slicing them into fillets was sort of an overdue revenge. I attacked the slimy creatures with zeal. The cook nodded and smiled approvingly.

As before several servants served the meal and others left for other duties. I managed to leave with those with tasks outside of the hall. When we all entered the bailey, I separated myself from the others and searched for Liam.

I looked in every merchant's stall and in the large storehouse. There was only one area I'd not sought the fox. The billet where the men-at-arms were housed.

It was near dark. I would have to hurry if I was to find Liam before the men settled in for the night. As the bailey was now empty I was less than vigilant.

"Looking for a soldier to share a pallet with, my lady?" A gruff voice pierced the silent darkness. He grabbed me and pressed his grimy hand over my mouth. Pushing me around the corner of the building, he forced me onto the ground.

~ ~ ~

LIAM

I thought I would fall immediately asleep but I was unable to. Something was wrong. I could feel it. It was a feeling quite foreign to me and it was a sensation far stronger than anything I'd felt before. A compulsion that could not be ignored.

Creeping from beneath the chair, I made certain I was alone in the throne room. The room was empty and as dark as ink. I followed the carpet to the door.

The only scent I could ascertain was from the kitchen fire: the loaves of bread left by the hearth to proof.

I went out into the bailey. Though faint, I picked up Chloe's scent. The sense of danger grew stronger. Every fiber of my being was attuned to Chloe and the danger she was in. She needed me and needed me now.

Her aroma led me to the soldier's billet. At this hour, one would assume the men within would all be sleeping. Yet something drew me to the men's quarters. Most of the men were in deep slumber, many snoring quite loudly.

Then I heard a muted cry and I noted two individuals engaged in a scuffle moving alongside the building. One struggling against the other. It was Chloe and she was putting up a heroic fight. She kicked, scratched, and butted her head against her attacker, who presented his back to me. I bit his rump just as hard and deep as the beast did me.

Finally Chloe brought her knee to his groin. He groaned and fell to the ground.

"Run!" I yelled.

She pulled herself up and headed for the door. Fortunately the fool was in no position to follow. Running as fleet as a deer, she was away in moments.

Luckily I can use my sense of smell over sight, for she'd run so fast she was completely out of view.

After what seemed like forever, I caught up to her. She didn't seem to be out of breath, but I was panting to catch my own.

"How do you move so swiftly?" I asked.

She laughed. "I just imagine I am swimming through the air as I did through the sea as a seal."

My heart sank. Was she so drawn to the sea that I can never truly be part of her life? She behaves as if she were freed from prison.

"Liam, I'm going swimming. It won't be as it was, but still very liberating."

I watched as she skipped to the water's edge. Throwing off her clothes, she walked into the sea until the water touched her thighs then she dove into an oncoming wave. Her arms cut the water like Viking oars. Further and further, she swam out into the open water.

"Don't go too far," I yelled, almost certain she couldn't hear me. Would she become so enamored of the life she once knew, that she would never return? I prayed not. I was certain in my heart we were destined to be together, yet my head hadn't received the message. *Chloe, come back. I need you.*

Sitting on the shore, I willed my faith to be stronger than my doubt.

~ ~ ~

CHLOE

This is so glorious. I've not felt this free since I can't remember when. It seems lonely here. The water is a balm to my soul. It caresses my body with a feel of the finest silk. This is the area where I once lived. Where is everyone?

I looked in each direction and saw no one. Then near the surface I glimpsed a flash of gold. It was Aggy and his golden horn.

"Chloe, Chloe, are you coming back for good?"

"Oh, as much as I would love to, I think fate has other plans for me."

"Please, please, we need you. Something is happening to the seals. Every day more are gone. It's bad, very bad."

"Does my Lord Neptune know of this?"

"He does, he does. He's sent me to warn the rest of the guys to go out to sea, into deeper water."

"Why?"

"Cause the traps are set in the shallows."

"Where? Show me."

Aggy swam ahead of me back toward the shore. Suddenly he was out of sight. I swam out a short ways to get a larger view and saw him in a hidden cove.

Never had I seen such a horrific scene. Line after line of traps. Larger than a lobster trap, but of the similar design, each was filled with a seal. Some dead, some dying, and many barking in agony. I had to free those I could and the torment that wrenched my soul was that I could not save them all. These were my people, my family.

In my haste to free them, I did not exercise caution. Pushing aside an empty trap to reach an injured seal, I tripped a trap and was caught myself.

"Aggy, flee, lest you, too, are caught. Tell Neptune and then go to the shore and tell Liam I am held captive."

I could see the little unicorn feared to leave me, but unless he got help here is where I perish.

Though the water muffled the sound, I could hear the screams of the captured seals. They were so frightened and there was nothing I could do that would calm their fear. Fortunately the traps floated once they were tripped so the poor creatures were able to breathe. How could I possibly free these poor souls? How can I save myself?

Suddenly, there was a strong drag on the line that held the traps, pulling us through the water. So rapidly it was hard to avoid the waves the movement created. We bounced along for what seemed like hours, though I am certain it was only minutes. Finally we were loaded on a lobster boat. The boat was large enough that all the traps were strung out in a row. Then I saw him. We were doomed, all of us. The man was Arwan, and he was well pleased with his catch.

"Well, well, what have we here? It's my little wifey. What were you doing swimming? You know that is against the rules. Now how shall I punish you? Beating does not seem to faze you, so how about no food? Would you like that, dear?"

"Stop, Arwan, what good comes of this? Why do you wish to kill every living thing that comes across your path? What are you doing with all these seals?"

"That's my business, Chloe, not yours. Rest assured I shall be well compensated for these water rats."

"You have me, I'll do whatever you want. Just let these seals free."

"I think not, my dear. As I said, their worth is quite large."

I was confused. These were not young seals who were often killed for their pelts, but seals of all ages many with so many scars their skins would be worthless. What was he doing with these poor animals? I know he is not going to allow them to live, but what can he be doing with them?

The traps skidded across the deck, clattering against the morning quiet. Gradually the morning progressed and more boats were fitted to go out to sea. Arwan waited until all the ships left the harbor before he released his catch. He took those dead first and bound them together. Then he did likewise to the dying. Finally he released those still alive and herded them into a shipping container. Me, he tied up tightly and bound to the mast. The seals' mournful barks pierced my heart. How could anyone not feel their pain?

~ ~ ~

LIAM

I followed Chloe's scent to the harbor in the dead of night. At first, the spores led me on a straight course, then for a time I was unable to smell her. But just before the dawn, I picked up her essence.

I walked carefully along the dock taking care that I would remain unseen. Hiding behind off-loaded cargo, I found myself led to a decrepit, putrid lobster boat. Eager to free my love, I unwisely rushed to board the boat. It was truly a foolhardy move, as Arwan spied me at once.

"Come here, you red rat."

I ran straight at him, through his legs, and eluded him. He was clearly angry as he stomped across the deck. There was no way he could catch me as I could hide in places he could not enter. Barrels were stacked on the deck three high, belly to belly. The shape of the barrels created small spaces between the casks. Small enough for a fox, but not large enough for a monster.

Even though I could get away from Arwan, there was little hope I could free Chloe by myself. My only hope was Murtaugh.

While Arwan was searching for me, I told Chloe I was going to get help.

Chapter 3

MURTAUGH

I truly don't know what to make of this situation. Neptune was unreachable, and the blind king doesn't care. How am I supposed to help in a solution when there is no one to aid?

It was getting near dusk, the time for Arwan to appear. Two very large stones on the deserted beach hid me from view of the cottage. I knew not of another place I could find those who would assist me.

It was fully dark and Arwan had not returned. Now the tide is coming in and I must move further up the beach. The never-ceasing tide moves and creates the pools little Aggy enjoys.

I heard a faint whinny to my left. I turned but saw no horse. It had to be Aggy in one of the tide pools. The whinny sounded more like danger than a greeting. Again I heard it, and this time it sounded frantic. I looked in each of the pools until I found him. He was panting as if he had been swimming a great distance.

"Good eve, Aggy, what has caused you to be short of wind?"
"Oh, Master Druid, it's the seals. He's killing them."
"Who is doing this dastardly thing?"
"Arwan, Chloe's ugly mean old husband. He's a bad guy."

Then, before I was even able to consider a solution, a bearded man appeared. He was wearing an old tweed jacket and a seaman's cap slung low over his forehead. His beard was as white as snow. Which was rather unusual as most facial hair is a combination of various hues. The closer he came, the more familiar he became.

He walked right up to me and took a long draw on the clay pipe in his mouth.

"What's the matter, Murtaugh, don't you recognize me?" Smiling, he exhaled a stream of white smoke.

"I didn't know you could come out of the sea."

"Why wouldn't I be able to do whatever I wish? I am a king, you know."

"Forgive me, Your Highness. Have you come to help me?"

Neptune winked and casually replied, "Well, I guess someone has to."

"Have you a plan? Do you know the cause for this grim darkness?"

"Not conclusively, but I have my suspicions."

"Would you care to share your suspicions? It would be good to know who we are up against."

"I don't have damning evidence but the man's demeanor leads me to believe he likes the situation just as it is."

"Who? What kind of a demented fool would want the entire land to be shrouded in darkness?"

"You might not like who I name, Murtaugh, but I know the King is one of our culprits."

"One of them? You mean this is a preconceived plan?"

"Yes, a conspiracy."

"Who? Who?"

"The king."

"You?"

The old man smiled widely. Apparently he was either amused or proud of his deduction. The Sea King was beside himself with laughter. He took off his cap and shoved it into his pocket.

"Not me, the blind king."

"Strangely that is not a surprise to me. When I met with him to discuss the situation, he offered nothing and left almost as soon as he arrived."

"Yeah, I know, a responsible regent he is not. He cares only for himself and his power."

"Then we must consider who can give him what he wants and what it is he wants more than anything."

Pondering the words of the Sea King, I began to pace, as I was my way of reaching viable conclusions. Up and down, back and forth, I walked for what seemed like hours. No matter how hard I thought, I could not come up with a reasonable explanation.

Neptune appeared to be totally unconcerned. He was leaning against a large rock smoking his pipe. Calm and relaxed as if he were in his own finely appointed library.

Frankly, I was somewhat piqued at his behavior. It was becoming apparent I was getting no help from any quarter. However, the Sea King's presence was comforting.

We moved together to sit upon some large rocks to plan our strategy.

I was concerned about who might have started this foul event. Feeling Neptune knew more about the situation than I did, I felt it wise to be the second to speak. Not rushing into the conversation was proving to be somewhat unsettling as I was impatient to proceed. Moreover, this tactic was pleasing to Neptune.

"My boy, I've been pondering this problem for some time now and I believe there is a solution. We cannot solve the problem alone. Chloe and the fox are integral. Without them we can achieve nothing."

"What do you mean? We're men. How would a woman and a woodland creature be able to do more than we?"

"Surely, Master Druid, a woman was at some point in your life able to completely confound you."

"Of course, when I was young and vulnerable. I'm wiser now."

"Are you really? I think a comely maiden could easily sway you."

"Perhaps, but I'm of no consequence at the moment. Let's get back to the problem at hand."

The bearded wise old man was teasing me, and I didn't appreciate it. Neptune smiled and rubbed his hands together.

"Now this is what I have observed. Somehow Chloe's husband and King Turlough are in this together. But neither of them has the brains to accomplish anything on a large scale. There has to be at least one other being to accomplish such a vast feat."

Ah, his nonchalance is a façade. He is thinking, planning. This turn of his behavior is more to my liking.

"Sire, if this be so, why don't we follow one of them until he meets with the other two? Perhaps we could learn something of their plans?"

The great King was stroking his long white beard as he was want to do whenever he was contemplating. *Neptune was carefully considering my suggestion. This pleases me. Now I am being valued.*

Both of us were so deep in thought we did not hear the fox running through the thicket without thought of stealth. He'd been racing for some time as he was panting to catch his breath. Liam stood before me, his head hung low, his tongue hanging from his mouth as he was trying to regain his wind.

The Sea King knelt beside him and stroked his head. "Calm yourself. We'll help you whatever the problem."

The fox shuddered and fell to the ground. I dropped to my knees and quickly examined him for injuries. There appeared to be none, yet something had happened to cause the poor animal to faint.

"Is he breathing?" Neptune asked.

"Yes," I replied, "I feel a faint pulse in his neck. What do you suppose caused him to collapse?"

"I'd say he's run some distance. He's probably exhausted."

The fox tried to stand, but he was too weak. Again he lay on the ground. As we were near the cottage and Arwan had not returned, I entered and searched Chloe's stores and found some willow bark. There was a pot over the fire that had a small amount of water that was tepid. I poured it into a cup, added the bark, and took it to the fox.

"Sire, how does he fare?"

"He's doing better, but is still a little shaky on his legs."

I brought the tea and bid the fox drink. He did so and coughed, as I made the concoction quite strong.

"What are you trying to do? Kill me? That liquid is foul." Neptune laughed.

"Woke you up though, didn't it, boy?"

"That it did, Your Highness. I've much to tell you."

"What is it, friend fox? Speak up, lad."

"I've found Chloe, but Arwan holds her prisoner."

The Sea King's nostrils flare. He drew his eyes to ominous slits and his face grew red. He was angrier than I'd ever seen him. His chest expanded and as he expelled his breath he was so incensed he shook. The massive fists were clenched, and he struggled to speak coherently.

"Where does the fiend hold her?"

"On his boat down at the harbor. He's been trapping seals and when Chloe tried to save them, she tripped a trap and was captured herself."

"Murtaugh, you come with me to the docks. Liam, find Aggy and tell him to send the seals even further out to sea."

The fox nodded and headed toward the tide pools while Neptune and I took off in the direction of the harbor.

~ ~ ~

LIAM

I approached the most distant tide pool and listened carefully for the whinny of the little golden horned seahorse. Though I held my breath not to miss the most faint of sounds, I heard no whinny, not even a nicker, only noisy sniffing and sobs.

"Aggy, Aggy, is that you? What's wrong?"

Sniffing, the little unicorn said, "It's the seals. Arwan has killed hundreds and now he has Chloe."

"He has Chloe? How?"

"When she went swimming, I found her and showed her the seal traps. She tried to free them and got caught herself."

"All right, you go to warn the seals and I'll see if I can find anything in the cottage to help her."

The tide was moving out quickly, leaving Aggy's pool surrounded by the beach pebbles. I reached into the pool and took him by his dorsal fin and walked him out into deeper water. He lifted a fin saying good-bye and dove beneath the surface.

I turned away from the shore and approached the cottage. Butting my head against the door was futile. All I was getting was a sore head. There had to be another way. I circled the building and found a window open a crack over a flowerbox. There was a bench beneath the opening. Jumping on the bench, I was able to climb into the flowers. I put my snout in the scant opening and pushed. It was hard work, but I had to help Chloe. I knew not how, but some way, sometime, somewhere we will be united. The feeling was so strong it motivated my every move.

Once I opened the glass enough to enter, I landed on a small table. What could there possibly be in here that can help her? Would Arwan injure her further? And if I find something how can I help her?

No sense wasting my time wondering how. I will accomplish this. It must be done.

~ ~ ~

MORIA

Damnation, I'm sick of being cooped up like a pigeon waiting to be sent on with a message. When? When is it my turn? When I married him he was outgoing, charming and his court was most spectacular. People were always visiting as we hosted frequent feasts. Food from all over the world. My mouth waters just thinking about it. Oh, how I miss those days.

Turlough was so generous before the loss of his sight. I have hundreds of exquisite ball gowns, but no one to wear them for. I can't even remember when I last danced.

There is no joy to be found in the dreary castle. This used to be the place where everyone who is anyone wished to be seen, but no longer.

My daydreaming was interrupted by my husband and his skinny ugly dog.

"Moria? Moria? Are you in here? Speak up, woman."

"I'm here, Turlough. Is there something you need?" Though he was no longer the man I married, he was still my husband. His dog walked toward me, teeth bared, and a low growl in her throat. The creature never liked me. Though I don't know why. I've always been fond of dogs, but this one was like a jealous, vindictive woman. The kind of female you never want to cross. Turlough seemed sad and contrite today, unlike his usual demeanor of bitterness.

"What troubles you, husband?"

"When? When will this foul contract be fulfilled? I am so sick of being blind. Damn your brother for his defiance, and damn me for speaking up for him. Damn, damn, we're all damned, all of us. Will we never be free?"

I took him in my arms and held him as I'd done when we first were wed. He leaned into me, seeking comfort, but I'd none to offer. He was right. We were doomed.

I'd been able to bargain with the devil when Arwan was defiant but there was no more room to negotiate. My brother suffered with his curse, but was unconcerned about the burdens thrust upon Turlough and me.

If Arwan had not been so greedy, we would have led normal lives. But no, he reasoned if he were consigned to be ugly he would have a comely wife.

It was not so long ago we entered than fiendish alliance. Orphaned, my brother Arwan and I were hungry, so very hungry. He built a trap to capture a seal. We could eat for many days from a single seal. But it was not as easy as we thought it would be.

We had not eaten in days when this very well-dressed man approached us carrying a full tray of food. It smelled so good. We raced to meet him.

He spoke in a deep and sonorous tone. "Are you hungry, my children?"

"We are, we are," we yelled.

"What would you do for me, if I make certain you never go hungry again?"

"Anything, anything, sir. What would you ask of us?"

"I need the souls of five thousand seals to fuel my fires."

I instantly became wary. How long, I wondered, would it take us to capture five thousand seals?

"Sir," I ventured, "Five thousand is a very large number. Could we not lower that amount?"

The man raised his eyebrows and nodded ever so slightly.

"I know that, lass. Call me Lucien and we might find a way, but it will require a longer commitment."

I grew increasingly concerned. How could I win in a game with the devil? I was convinced this Lucien was, in fact, the devil himself.

My ever-impetuous brother rushed at him and shoved him in the chest. At once, the impeccably dressed devil's eyes started glowing red and a thin line of acrid smoke emerged from his ears. Arwan appeared to be paralyzed and his body became covered with fur. His feet became hooves and his head was that of a snake. A forked tongue emerged from his maw. Arwan was now a Questing Beast.

Somehow I had to make this better. "My Lord Lucien, could you please temper your punishment? Perhaps make him beast like only when the sun disappears?"

"My Lord Lucien? I like that. In deference to your courtesy, I will comply."

Chapter 4
....

LIAM

I poked my nose in every nook and corner I saw, and found nothing. The only space left to search was the funny-looking cabinet by the door.

The edges of the door opening were jagged, like teeth, and the pulls were at the top of the cabinet.

I pushed the table next to it and climbed up in order to reach the knobs. They were very close to each other. I turned my head to the side that I might grasp a single knob and pulled. Nothing happened. I looked at the small space between the doors. It was not an opening, only a saw cut to make it appear as if it were. Puzzled and frustrated, I grabbed both knobs with my teeth firmly and pulled with every bit of strength in me. As I tugged the entire front yielded. Not as one would expect, but what seemed as doors was a single piece. The hinge was at the base. As the panel opened it pushed back the table and left me hanging from the knobs I clenched in my teeth. I let go, falling to the floor, and out rolled a small gray bundle. Though seals are not my usual prey, the scent was unmistakable.

I'd found Chloe's skin!

~ ~ ~

MURTAUGH

The eyesight of the King of the Sea is nothing short of astounding. Though we were close to the pier I could not discern exactly who was aboard Arwan's boat, but Neptune saw Chloe and a group of live seals on the deck. He said the girl and the seals were somehow connected to one another.

"Neptune, how can we free her and protect the seals? We have no weapons."

"Ah, friend Druid, you are incorrect. We have at our command some of the most powerful weaponry in the world."

"We do? Where?"

The great sea king rose to his full height, smiled widely, and spoke in a mocking tone.

"I told you I'm a king and my subjects are loyal."

"I understand, Your Highness, your subjects are loyal, but what does that have to do with weapons?"

"You will see, my friend. Come, we have to get to the cottage before the tide goes out."

We raced back to the cottage. I don't think I've run that much since I was six. I was totally out of breath when we reached our destination.

I know a certain reverence is required for a king, but Neptune vacillates between extreme authority and humility, so it is difficult to know how to respond to him. The Sea King is presently in complete charge. All will obey him. He let out a strong shrill whistle and mere moments passed before a huge pod of dolphins congregated just off shore.

They stood on their tails, in a precise line facing their king. Neptune then emitted several whistles of different tones. At once, in a specific order, they turned in a complete circle, then dove into deeper water.

"Your Highness," I ventured, "What did you tell them?"

"They are bringing out the big guns."

~ ~ ~

ARWAN

Those fools think they can best me, they are sorely mistaken. Not only did I see them, I can see just what they plan on doing. Trying to run me aground will do no good. I know they've left to rally their forces, but I will be far out to sea before they can gather soldiers.

I will always get the best of the deal. I'm far more cunning than that damned fox that always shows up at the wrong time. I've made the best of the cursed contact so far and I will get all the demon promised and more he had not planned on giving me. I turned and looked at my greatest prize: my wife. It hurts me I must treat her thus, but in time she will understand.

She looked so forlorn laying on the blood-soaked deck. Her sobs rent my soul, but there is nothing I could do about it. It is well past time I would usually be in port and going home to one of her savory meals, but it can't be helped. I must remain in the deep waters until I can get the cargo to the bog. The red sky portends a gray day, not that all of them aren't.

At once the sea began to roil with the onslaught of hundreds of diving and surfacing dolphins. The sea looked like a boiling pot, thousands of bodies creating a choppy sea. Higher and higher the waves rose until I was unable to see the crest of the next one. It slammed onto the deck and threatened to swamp us. The seals were thrown to the stern and washed into the churning sea. Another, yet higher, wave washed over the deck taking Chloe with it. She bobbed on the water like a discarded cork. And then, as if it had never happened, the water became as calm as a placid pool. The surface smooth as a mirror, the dolphins were gone, the seals were gone, and Chloe appeared to have vanished completely. My heart wrenched as I saw her washed overboard. I wish I could have left her with some redeeming thoughts of me, but it was not to be.

There was little sense of me trying to get to the bog with an empty boat. I grabbed the tiller and headed for the cottage. I would get little sleep, knowing Chloe is gone and my sister still has her wishes unfulfilled. The two of us had weathered many a tempest, but this may prove to be the final blow.

I'm certain Lucien will chastise me greatly. He is quite formidable when angered. I no longer fear of him, as he knows he needs me more than I need him. Taking the brunt of his anger was fine with me as long as Moria was safe. I'd promised our father I would make sure she married well and have every advantage. If it weren't for my oath, we would still be living by the sea and I would be a regular fisherman, not the murderer of hundreds of seals.

I had to head out to sea a ways so I could navigate the channel into the harbor. What I saw curdled my blood. Boats already moored were washed high upon the shore, so far from the water there was no way they could simply float again. Looking back into the sea, I could see the cause for this disaster. Two of the largest whales I had ever seen were raising their bodies into the air then slamming down on the surface. The waves were monstrous, so high as to nearly obliterate the sky. I don't frighten easily, but this had me shaking in my boots. I was certain I would not emerge victorious, if, in fact, I were able to emerge at all. There was nothing left on my boat. I was thrown fore and aft, then starboard, next port. My blood was joining that already on the deck. The crimson tide washing toward me, then retreating. What I felt was far beyond fear. Worse than feeling you were just this side of hell, knowing where you would end up would be the most outer reaches of the foul place. There was no way I could survive. But still I struggled on.

Someone had to save Moria, and I was the only one who could. This deal with the devil must come to fruition. The devil has his due, now it is time for him to honor his debt.

~ ~ ~

LIAM

Carrying the seal pelt, I stepped out of the cottage. Neptune and Murtaugh were kneeling beside Aggy's pool. They seemed extraordinarily joyous. *Do they not realize we are in a dire situation?*

Aggy is laughing so hard he is creating ripples in the shallow water. *What's wrong with these fools?* Have they forgotten Chloe? And what about the *problem*? The damned gray pall that covers the entire land? Have they been drugged? I dropped the pelt.

"Hey!" I shouted.

"What's wrong with you idiots?"

The men rose and rushed toward me. Murtaugh grabbed me up saying, "We've come through this. Liam, Arwan is defeated. We just need to find the bog and figure a way to shut it down."

"That's great, but have you forgotten Chloe? She's more important to me than any bog."

Neptune turned and ordered Murtaugh to set me on the ground. My feet no more than touched the dirt, when Neptune raged, "How dare you? You have no reason to accuse me of not caring for my subjects. They are my primary concern."

I was beyond fearing the wrath of the Sea King. Chloe was more than just one of his subjects. She was mine, my soul mate. We were destined to be together. I will dare anything, everything, for this regent to save her.

"Calm down, friend fox. She's safe," Neptune replied, knowing my concern was for Chloe.

"How can you know that? She was on Arwan's boat. If he's dead, what happened to Chloe? What about all those poor seals?"

The King knelt beside me and shook his head. "Unfortunately we have lost a great number of seals but those on Arwan's boat are still alive as is Chloe."

"You're certain she's alive? Where is she?"

"The big guns are bringing her here."

Murtaugh clasped his hands in prayer and rolled his eyes toward heaven.

Suddenly I heard a series of whistles and clicks. The surface of the water roiled as a large group of seals came swimming toward us. The sea churned, as active as a boiling pot of stew. As astounding as the creatures, what came next was beyond belief: two of the largest whales I could ever have imagined. The entire horizon was obliterated by the massive beasts. Riding the crests of the waves created by the seals, the swimming mammals came closer.

Neptune stepped into the sea and assumed his god-like stature. Nearly the size of the two whales, the King of the Deep raised his arms and laughed, a deep, full, hearty bellow. A sound so loud it reverberated off the beach, causing the pebbles to dance.

"My friends allow me to introduce you to my formidable arsenal. On my right is Maximo and on my left is my oldest and most experienced, Colossus. No boat has escaped them unscathed."

These were the largest of any beast I'd ever seen. Strangely I was not frightened, especially when I noticed Chloe atop Colossus. She was cradling Arwan in her arms. Why would she care for him? He'd been unspeakably cruel to her and had never offered her a single tender word. Her compassion was far greater than mine would ever be for such a fiend. She was crying, deep, heaving sobs. It was becoming clear the man she held was in his death throes.

~ ~ ~

CHLOE

"Please, Arwan, save your strength," I begged him. Though he was an evil entity, he was also my husband. I did not love him as such, but I've great compassion for those held in the grasp of foul contracts with the devil. I knew he'd made such a bargain that his sister would be well cared for a provided with more than he could give her.

He pulled me toward him and said, "I'm not the best husband, devil tormented me." I tried to get him to be silent, but to no avail. "Bog in wood. Go put out fires. It's the only way he can be thwarted." He clasped my hand tightly and struggled to catch his breath. I bid him to be quiet, but he did not heed me. He drew in a great breath and again spoke in a single bursting sentence. "If even a single spark left, he will escape and all will be lost.

Protect my sister." He gasped, and a trickle of blood fell from his mouth and he was no more.

Colossus sank just enough for me to get onto the dock carrying Arwan's body. I found it somewhat strange that such a large animal could have such compassion. He seemed to sense my opposing emotions. He then dove deep into the sea and Maximo came alongside the pier.

Liam rushed to my side. "Are you injured? Why are you holding Arwan's body so tenderly, after all he did to you? We must leave this is no longer the land it once was. Please, Chloe, come away with me."

"As dearly as I wish I could, I cannot. I must honor Arwan's last wish."

"Why? Why would you even care?"

My Liam was puzzled with what seemed to be a vast change in my demeanor. He did not understand. At the end, Arwan died a good man.

"All the evil he did was done for his sister. It was always just him and his sister. The two of them against a very cruel life. They were orphaned at her birth and Arwan swore to his dying mother he would care for his sister. She is the reason he made the deal with the devil: that his sister marry well and was provided her every wish. What happened to me was incidental. His rages were not against me, but Satan."

There was a large carriage coming toward us. It was a beautifully appointed conveyance. When it came to a stop, a very beautiful young woman emerged. She saw me at once and began to wail. It had to be Arwan's sister. No one else would have cared enough to mourn. The poor lass was wracked with the pain of losing her brother. Trying to contain herself she came to me and tried to take Arwan's body from me. The man was dead weight and she fell to the ground holding him in her arms

"Arwan, whatever it takes I will see you are avenged. All the torment you have suffered for me will not go unnoticed."

I knelt beside her and placed my arm around her shoulders. Murtaugh eased the dead man from her grasp. "I know you have never met me, but I was his wife. Our marriage was not happy but in the end your brother was a good man and he cared deeply for you. He's told me where to find the bog and how to thwart Lucien."

"How? The man is the very devil himself. And where is that man taking my brother?" she said, pointing at Murtaugh as he was walking away.

"I don't know exactly, but trust me he will be treated with reverence until we seal the bog."

I heard a loud click coming from the carriage. The door opened, and a very thin tall dog stepped out followed by an ornately dressed man, using a large cane to tap the area around him as he held tightly to the dog's harness.

"Moria, Moria?" he cried, turning in every direction, frantically trying to locate the lass.

"I'm right here, Turlough, straight in front of you."

"Thank the fates. I thought I'd lost you. I am nothing without you. What has happened? Why were you crying?"

"Turlough, Arwan is dead."

"Dead? What will happen to us? If he cannot honor his debt to Lucien, I'll be blind forever."

"Fear not, my love, he left instructions for us to free ourselves from the Devil's wrath."

I was somewhat piqued that the poor fool only thought of himself.

Chapter 5

MURTAUGH

Maximo was gently tapping his tail fluke on the surface of the water, clearly impatient to get on with the task at hand. He slowly lowered his body to the edge of the landing platform and whistled for us to board.

Liam rushed up to me, asking, "What will happen to Chloe? Will I forever remain a fox?"

I had no answer to the lad's question, yet I knew that we all had been chosen for an important mission and would most likely be well compensated and was equally certain the reward would not be monetary. "Fear not, friend fox, the High Council will see all matters will be put to rights."

The poor animal's demeanor sunk. It was as if he took to the ocean's depths. I looked around and noted Neptune was no longer present. Why would he desert us at such a time as he would be most needed? Sometimes that man infuriates me. How he ever got to be king is beyond my comprehension. He appears and disappears without thought of the situation he is impacting.

Now I had another "King" to deal with. Turlough was no more a perfect regent than Neptune. The poor blind fool thinks too much about his own issues and far too little about the needs of his subjects. The man is now blubbering on his wife's shoulder. I dare say she has shouldered much of the burden of his kingdom. I only pray he is aware of her sacrifice. They seem to be comforting each other. Perhaps there is hope for them after all? I walked toward them intending to overhear their conversation. I needed to know the status of group before I delegated tasks. If Turlough was so self-involved, he would be useless. However, it seems there is some change in both the man and his wife. As if they had suddenly grown back bones. There was a quiet strength about them. Liam noticed as well. He was circling my legs trying to gain my attention.

"Murtaugh, are you coming with us? Maximo knows the way to the bog and Chloe is aboard his back along with the King and Queen. They have much to tell you. Please come, we need your wisdom."

Maximo is becoming impatient, rocking his body side to side creating waves that cause the dock to sway.

"I'm coming, you massive beast. Hold steady."

He ceased his rocking and held firm that I might board. Liam jumped into my arms, and I stepped onto the back of the huge whale.

Liam lay contented in my arms for most of the voyage, yet when we got close to the bog, he became agitated, as his strong sense of smell told him the bog was near. He yipped to warn the others to cover their mouths else they would choke on the noxious fumes. Leaping from my arms, he ran to Chloe, who was so upset she inhaled and nearly fainted. I caught her, and Liam rushed to her side as I lowered her to the ground. He licked her face trying to rouse her.

The stronger the stench, the nearer the foul pit. I knew we were near our goal. If only the blind King and his wife did not do something foolish. I knew I could trust the fox and his love, but I was unsure of the royal pair.

As the smell becomes unbearable the ground begins to shake, the trees shudder, even the sky trembles. I glanced back from whence we came and saw Neptune. Strangely he was the massive size I thought was his, only in the sea.

It was clear the regent was angry. But angry was too mild a word to describe the great Sea King's demeanor. He raged, thrashing through the trees as he did the seas.

Though his fury was great, he turned and winked at me. Sending a message that he was not losing his temper but was using it. The louder he raged, the more convinced I became that there would be a good ending to this confrontation.

Glancing to the shore, I noted the Blind King's carriage was keeping pace with the whale. As Maximo wove through the twists and turns of the channel the carriage maneuvered every turn. Maximo pulled up to the dock as the Queen halted the carriage.

Neptune rushed ahead of us spewing great volumes of sea water. The salt water covered the surface creating a cap of pure salt and smothered the foul flames. The final tendrils dwindled and the conflagration appeared to be contained. His task completed, he simply was gone. Where?

Moria leapt from the royal conveyance, threw her arms wide, and danced with abandonment. Her husband sat dejectedly in the driver's seat, his head in his hands.

~ ~ ~

CHLOE

"Liam." I sobbed into his soft fur. How I wished I could tell him of my true feelings. Of how important he is to me. But first we must attend to duty. The King of the Oceans must be found.

"Come, it is up to us to find Neptune." Liam wiggled in my arms. I sensed he feared he couldn't breathe beneath the water.

"Don't fear I will help you breathe."

"How? I am not a sea creature."

"But I am, and I will let nothing harm you." He relaxed as we neared the beach. The tide was out so we would have to go further into the sea deep enough to swim.

The water was cold, but the chill was more in my heart than my limbs. We had to find Neptune, else we all would perish. And mayhap our land would not be the only one so effected.

I held Liam in my arms and placed my mouth over his muzzle and forced air into his lungs. He looked up at me trust in his gaze. I nodded, affirming I felt the same.

We were quite a ways into the ocean, when I heard the whistle of dolphins join with the soft bark of seals. The sound was mournful and seemed to grow in volume as more and more seals and dolphins lent their voices to the lament.

Though tears are not easily seen in the sea, the expression upon the face of Neptune showed the depth of his sorrow. The King addressed the ever- growing crowd. Joining the seals and dolphins were creatures of every species in the sea.

Though his eulogy was beautiful and heartfelt, we needed to leave, else the land would be host to many, many more funerals.

I walked to the podium and gently placed my hand on the King's arm.

Somberly he looked down at me, saying, "I know, Chloe, I'm coming."

Liam pushed against my legs. Clearly he needed my breath yet again. I forced air into his lungs and Neptune petted his head, then he was able to breathe without my aid. The poor fox was astounded. He swam around me, then toward the open sea, elated with his new freedom. The Sea King reached out and grabbed Liam by the tail.

"Not so fast, my furry friend. Now is not the time for play. We must attend to duty. I have a feeling if we accomplish ridding the land of this horrific evil, we all will be rewarded far beyond our greatest dreams."

Liam bowed his head before Neptune, who acknowledged his respect. Once again the master of the sea grew to massive size and held both of us, one under each arm. Together we moved far faster than I ever swam. Within moments we were back at the ship.

Murtaugh was pacing the deck, the Blind King and his wife sobbing in each other's arms.

At least some good has come from this mess. At least the blind King and his Queen were depending on themselves instead of constantly whining that another serve them.

As Neptune placed his feet on shore, he regained a more human stature as he placed us on the ground. The three of us walked up the gangway.

Neptune tapped Murtaugh on the shoulder and asked, "What has transpired since I left?"

~ ~ ~

MURTAUGH

Well, the great man has returned. I was more than a little angered with Neptune. His appearances and disappearances were more disconcerting than I felt I should have to deal with. According to the Council this was to be a team effort. It definitely was not a group undertaking. A fox, a selkie, a blind man, and a deity who is gone, then reappears willy-nilly. Hardly a group of experts.

"Well, my liege, so nice to see you again."

"I have duties, Druid," he responded tersely. He did not like being chastised no matter how concealed the jibe.

"Again," I said, "What has transpired in my brief absence?"

"Though you extinguished the majority of the flames, I fear even a tiny tendril of smoke could bring back the entire conflagration. The royals are crying in their carriage. Chloe and Liam have just returned with you. What am I to do with the whining regents? I am certain the Council expected I would have aid in this endeavor."

"And so you shall, Murtaugh. Much more than you might have expected."

~ ~ ~

LUCIEN

These fools think I can be bested with a single wave? Though water is a great extinguisher, oil is not, and seal flesh contains much oil. Even now it floats skimming over the water in search of a tiny spark.

There beside that ancient oak a minuscule flame reaches gallantly for air and an accelerant. Ah, fire, you are such a pretty princess.

I moved my foot splashing the oil to the flame. Success. The small princess has become a raging queen. It shall not take long, soon the seal pit will burn once more. The stench and smoke will keep the land in darkness as my master wishes. *Nothing can stop me now.* He will have his souls, and I shall be amply rewarded. *All is well.*

However there must be measures taken to insure I will prevail. I placed my foot at the edge of a pool of oil and herded it to the edge of a willow branch. The flame of the oil sputtered with the moisture from the leaf, but I directed the flame until it roared to life. Smoke was now covering the landscape. *I couldn't be happier.*

~ ~ ~

LIAM

Though we were not close to the pit, I smelled burning and the sky was beginning to darken. My ears pricked as I heard the sound of a growing conflagration.

I let out a growl that was nearly a roar. *We're doomed!*

All eyes turned to me, then they looked to the skies and concluded the same as me. Only Neptune seemed unconcerned. Didn't he realize in time his world too would be annulated?

The mighty king once again rose to his massive stature. And from behind him an even greater gargantuan wave swept around and over the regent.

Instantly, Neptune grabbed up the three of us and the blind king's carriage and held us safely in his arms.

As the water slightly receded, I saw the whales Maximo and Colossus head for deeper waters. Once they reached the depths they sought, one after another they turned creating another wave the like of which I have never see in a lifetime.

It enveloped the King of the Sea then carried him and his burden to the crest as it covered the entire land.

There we stood as if frozen in place on the crest of the giant wave. It seemed time was passing in slow motion, each minute stretching into an hour, the hours into days.

~ ~ ~

LUCIEN

This cannot be happening. How did he do that? It was to have been my crowning achievement.

All is lost.

I can feel my strength waning. I am melting. The marrow in my bones is becoming molten. My limbs are like rubber. No longer can I stand.

And there he stands, muscular arms enfolding his comrades. That one spark was to have been my salvation, snuffed out as easily as a candle in a summer breeze.

Nothing will be left of me. No triumph, no glory only nothing. I have nothing, am nothing, and forever nothing will be my legacy. I wept bitter tears, the sorrow encompassing my entire body.

All is for naught!

~ ~ ~

CHLOE

How long have we been held here in suspension? It must have been quite a while as I have seen the sunset thrice. Yet I feel no discomfort from being in the same position for days.

I looked around and noticed some feeling coming into my limbs. I turned and saw Liam stretch and shake himself all over. The Blind King and his wife emerged from the carriage moving about to regain feeling in their limbs.

Suddenly, the darkened skies became infused with light. And from the heavens came the Council dressed in regal raiment. They came down the beam as if they were sliding down a hill. So unused to such a brilliant light we all shielded our eyes. I don't know how it happened, but though I felt no movement it appeared we were on the ground.

Neptune, now the size of a human man, smiled widely at the Council. "Ladies and gentlemen, welcome to our realm. We have done as you directed. Are we to be compensated?"

A very solemn voice intoned, "Surely you do not expect coin for doing only that which is right?"

Humbled, we all, save Neptune, replied, "No, most revered Council."

Neptune alone refrained from affirmation. He held silent, but glowered at the beings before him.

The tallest of the Council members stared at the King. "Well, man, speak up. What is it you think you are due?"

"Not I, but those who suffered and served you surely should be relieved of their pain and torment?"

The Council gathered themselves into a small cluster to confer. From time to time, one, then another would look up from their conclave to stare at us.

I held Liam in my arms, wishing somehow we could be mated. I longed for this and this alone. I'd little use for coin. Other than the love I desired, I lacked for nothing.

The tall thin man who appeared to be the leader of the Council stepped from the group with his hands clasped before him.

"After careful consideration, we the Council deem your request reasonable."

~ ~ ~

NEPTUNE

Humph, deem my request reasonable, do you? Do you think it is an easy task to rule the oceans? Getting those whales to do what you required was far from a simple task. It wasn't like you could simply talk to them. They communicate with an unusual song. Very difficult to duplicate. However arguing with you isn't going to get me what I want.

"And what sort of reward does the Council propose?" I inquired.

The thin man cleared his throat. "You do understand we cannot wave a magic wand and all will be aright?"

Clearly they were going to put us through some sort of test. I sighed and answered them as calmly as possible. "It is understood. What are we to do?"

The thin man let out the breath he'd been holding. He was intimidated. And why wouldn't he be? If I choose, I can be twenty times larger than he. I could crush him like an insect. Again, he cleared his throat and summoned the courage to present the tests to me.

Murtaugh the Druid must record and protect all happenings of this incident. The document will be hidden and the recovery of it should it become lost will be solely your responsibility.

Moria and Thurlough are to bring their kingdom to prosperity within a single year. Should they be successful, Thurlough will regain his sight and Moria shall have a child.

Aggy will continue to act as royal liaison between the sea and the land. He will be able to walk on land and swim the seas. Upon the ground he will be a pony and within the water a seahorse. He will sacrifice his golden horn to Thurlough to assist him in restoring his regency.

If he does not return to the sea before dusk, Aggy will forever be a pony. If he remains in the sea for more than two days a seahorse forever shall he be.

Mighty Neptune, you have ruled your domain justly and have well provided for your subjects. Your tasks will be to instruct the Blind King to do the same. Should you fail you will have to deal with the trials of forever being one size.

Chloe must decide if she wishes to be a seal, a mermaid, or a human woman.

Liam has a similar decision. He must determine if he would be a merman or remain a fox.

"These are your tasks, go forth and perform."

Chapter 6
....

MURTAUGH

As if I was never responsible for the hundreds of documents I've copied over the years.

I've never failed before, why does the Council need to test me? I've been faithful to my duties as a Druid. They have no right to question my abilities.

I left the group and went high into the hills to the cave known only to me. It was here I labored many years over hundreds of pages. I am responsible for centuries of oral history. And I have done so faithfully for many eons.

~ ~ ~

MORIA

"Oh, Turlough, you will see once again. I am so pleased."

"And you shall have a babe.

"'Tis truly wonderful. We shall be a family." Turlough smiled weakly at me and sighed.

"Yes, this could come to fruition save for the fact I have no idea how we can prosper."

"Dear husband, I see those who care for others more than themselves have a happier countenance than those who do nothing but wait to be served."

"Are we to be as villains and served them their meals?"

Smiling, I replied, "No, not serve meals but do our best to provide for those within our kingdom. Make certain our crops will feed them.

Our wool will clothe them and we will provide entertainments to put joy in their hearts."

"Ah, I understand but how are we to do this?" My still-skeptical husband inquired.

"On the morrow we shall a rise with the sun and go to the village and learn the needs of our subjects."

Worry still crossed the features of my beloved. He raised his head and a single tear slid down his cheek. "I know, Moria. I, too, would like to see to our subjects needs but there is far too little left in the treasury."

I gathered him into my arms. "Did you not hear the Council say Aggy is to give us his golden horn. I'm sure it is worth a great deal."

His smile changed his entire presence. "Yes, yes, I remember, and didn't they direct the Mighty Neptune to instruct us?"

~ ~ ~

AGGY

Wow, what a boon. Unless I am foolish I can see no loss for me. Do as I am bid, and I shall have the best of both worlds. I shall sleep in the bed of the seas and gallop the meadows during the day.

I am still to be the bridge between the waters and the land.

~ ~ ~

NEPTUNE

"How do you dare? I've ruled the Seven Seas for centuries. I'm a fair and just regent. My size is within my purview not yours." I bellowed to get my message across. The thin man shook but said nothing.

"I will gladly aid the Blind King and I will not fail. If there is fault to be found it shall rest on his head not mine."

~ ~ ~

CHLOE

I held Liam tightly in my arms and pressed my face into his soft fur. To feel his heartbeat against mine was sheer joy. The feeling of loving and being loved was far greater than mere words can describe.

Suddenly, he pushed against my grasp.

"Chloe, what we have been offered is not acceptable to me," he said, squirming until I released him.

He ran from me as his paws hit the ground. Headed for the nearest thicket, he was gone from my sight in moments. I followed him, hoping he would realize he is mistaken about the wisdom of our choices.

As I neared the wood, he emerged, growling at me with his teeth bared. "Liam, Liam, please tell me. What is it about our choices that troubles you?"

"You were given three choices. I was given only two."

"Are you desirous of an option you were not offered?"

"I know you want to be a human woman. My feelings for you urge me to want to be a human man to your woman."

I bristled at his conclusion. I'd never said I want to be a woman. "Liam, calm yourself. I do not want to be a woman and live on land. I never even entertained the idea."

He sat on his haunches then went down even further and crossed his paws over his muzzle.

"Why? Why? Wouldn't you want to be human? You could wander through the meadows, travel wherever you wish."

"I don't wish to run or travel. I want to swim, to be free, where no one seeks to kill me."

"So you wish to be a seal?"

I shook my head vehemently. "Being a seal is only part-time living. As a seal I would be part of the food chain."

"So you would be a mermaid?"

"Yes, and you should become a merman. We will be a family."

"I will not spend my life with a mate who does not love me."

"Not love you? Oh, Liam, I've loved you long and well, from the moment my eyes first beheld you."

Then, side by side, together we walked into the sea.

~ ~ ~

LUCIEN

Think you've bested me, fools? I've saved the fumes and from them I shall arise again. I will prevail, evil has no time limit.

Gentle reader, so closes this chapter in the never-ending battle between good and evil.

To thwart evil, we must place our wants behind the needs of others and keep faith that goodness will endure.

Before you leave this Fox Tale, please leave a review on www.amazon.com. And do come to my website www.deecareybooks.com and learn what is coming next to the world of foxes. Thank you. I hope you enjoyed the tale as much as I enjoyed writing it.

Also from **Dee Carey** and in **Writers' Branding:**

FOX TALES

Two Tales of Love

Mark of the Fox

Can an enchanted fox and a scarred prince follow the predestined course the Druids have set for them? They fight against the constraints of royalty, but in the end the falconer becomes a willing regent and the fox, his more- than-willing wife.

The Fox and the Swan

To save her family, a girl becomes a swan. The man she loves is enchanted by a witch into a fox. Can the pair unite as humans and save her family? True love triumphs over evil with the aid of a druid, a bishop, and a goddess.

Available on Amazon.

THE CRIMSON VIXEN

The preordained couple meet when Leigh discovers an orphaned fox and keeps her as a secret companion. In time it is revealed his Kit is also a fierce female pirate. The Druids determine the pair are destined to rule Ireland. As a fox she is clever. As a woman she is enchanting. Can Leigh set aside his devotion to King Arthur to be with the woman of his dreams?

Available on Amazon.

FOX TALES II

Two tales will enchant and bring to you the joy of magic, faith, courage, and the most powerful force in the universe: Love

Can Sean save himself and his friends from the grasp of the most foul? Can Merlot and LaRoux follow their preordained paths to save church and country?

Available on Amazon.

www.ingramcontent.com/pod-product-compliance
Lightning Source LLC
LaVergne TN
LVHW041542060526
838200LV00037B/1094